This Book Belongs To

_____

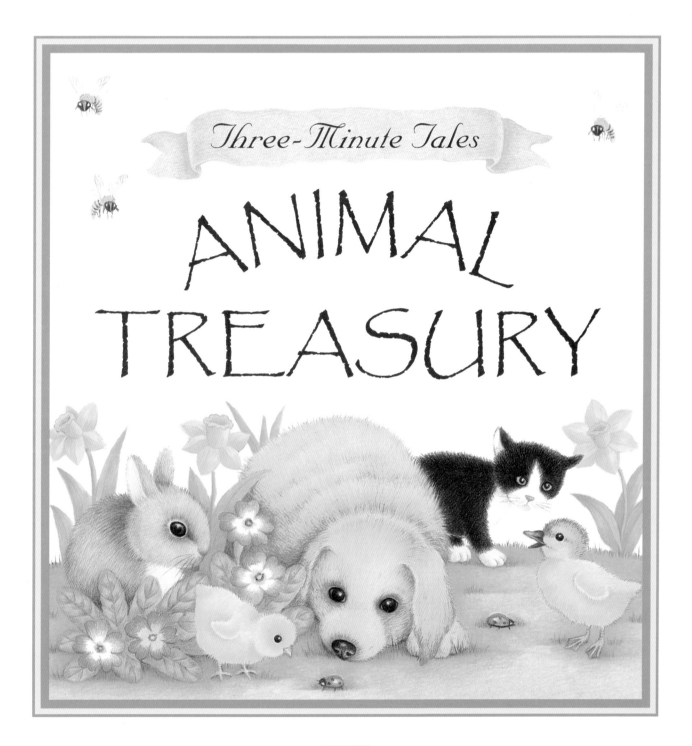

Three-Minute Tales

ANIMAL
TREASURY

p

This is a Parragon book
This edition published in 2001

Parragon
Queen Street House, 4 Queen Street,
Bath, BA1 1HE, UK

Produced by The Templar Company plc
Pippbrook Mill, London Road, Dorking,
Surrey, RH4 1JE, UK

Designed by Kilnwood Graphics

Printed and bound in Spain
ISBN 0-75253-604-4

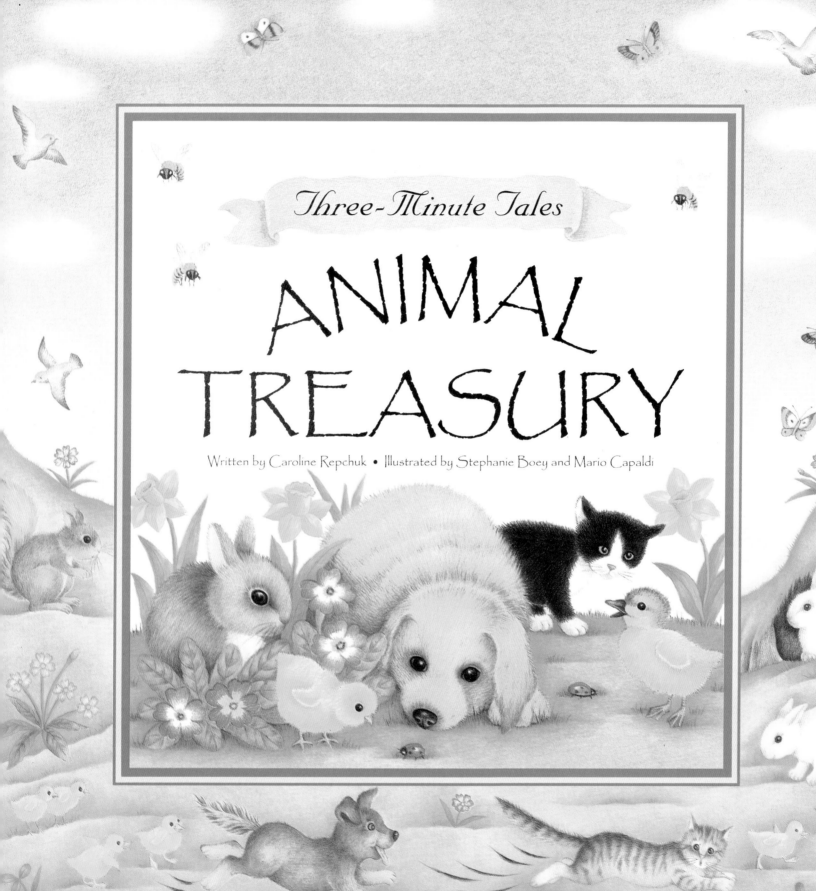

Three-Minute Tales

ANIMAL
TREASURY

Written by Caroline Repchuk • Illustrated by Stephanie Boey and Mario Capaldi

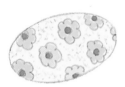

CONTENTS

Danny Duckling in Trouble

All at Sea!

Forever Friends

Like a Duck to Water!

Smelly Pup
Chasing Tails
Puppy Playtime
Bone Crazy!
One Stormy Night

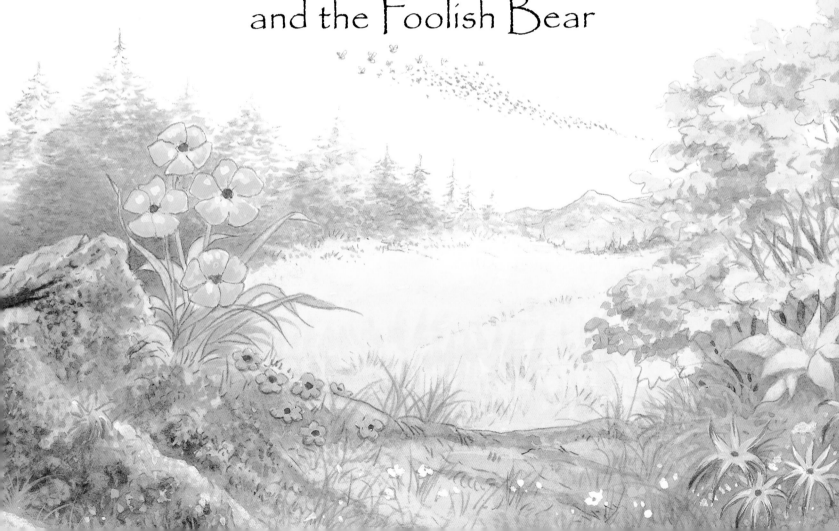

CHICKS

In spring time, fluffy yellow chicks hatch out from the eggs which their mothers have been sitting on, keeping them warm in the nest.

The chicks' sharp little beaks break open
the egg shells, and they step out into a cosy
bed of hay, eager to explore all the exciting
sights and sounds of the farmyard.

LITTLE CHICK LOST

"Stay close, Little Chick!" said Mummy, as they set out to visit Mrs Duck, who lived on the pond. Little Chick tried to keep up with Mummy, but there were so many interesting things to look at that he soon got lost in the long grass.

He was busy watching a shiny beetle climb a stem of grass, when a dark shadow fell over him. Little Chick looked up to see a huge dribbling mouth coming towards him!

It was a hungry fox! "Help!" he cried,
looking around for somewhere to hide.

Just then, Spot, the farm dog, appeared and
with a great woof he chased the fox away.
He was good at protecting the farm animals.
Mummy arrived flapping her wings.
"I told you to stay close," she said, tucking
Little Chick under her wing. And from then
on, that is just where Little Chick stayed!

THE DISAPPEARING EGGS

Mrs Hen had been sitting on her nest for
a long time, and she was tired and uncomfortable.
"I wish these eggs would hurry up and hatch!"
she said to herself, crossly. But all she could
do was sit and wait, so she closed her eyes
and soon fell fast asleep.

She dreamt she was sitting on her nest when all of a sudden it started to wobble and shake. She was tipped this way, and that, being poked and prodded as the eggs moved beneath her - someone was stealing her eggs! A deep voice was saying, "What lovely big ones!" It must be Mr Fox! She had to save her eggs!

Mrs Hen woke with a start, and looked
down at her nest in alarm. Sure enough,
her eggs had disappeared - but in their
place were six fluffy chicks, all prodding her
with their sharp little beaks.

"What lovely big ones!" said a deep voice nearby. It was Old Ned, the donkey. "Aren't they just!" said Mrs Hen with relief. "They were certainly worth the wait!"

MAKING A SPLASH!

One day, Mrs Hen and her chicks were
walking near the pond when Mrs Duck
swam by, followed by a line of ducklings.
The ducklings splashed around ducking
and diving in the water. "Can we play in
the water too?" the chicks asked Mrs Hen.
"It looks like fun!"

"Oh, no, dears," said Mrs Hen. "Chicks and water don't mix!" This made the chicks very miserable. "It's not fair!" they grumbled. "We wish we were ducklings!"

On the way home, a big black cloud appeared and it started to rain. Soon the chicks' fluffy feathers were wet through.

They scurried back to the henhouse as fast as they could and arrived wet, cold and shivering. Soon they were snuggled in the cosy warm straw, and their feathers were dry and fluffy again.

"Imagine being wet all the time!" said the chicks. "Thank goodness we're not ducklings, after all!"

CHEEKY CHICK

Cheeky Chick was a playful little chick. He was always playing tricks on his brothers and sisters. He would hide in the long grass, then jump out on them in surprise, shouting "Boo!" One day they decided to get their own back. "Let's play hide and seek," they said.

They left Cheeky Chick to count to ten,
while they all went to hide. Cheeky Chick
hunted high and low for his brothers
and sisters. He looked in all his favourite

hiding places but they were nowhere to be found. "Come out," he called. "I give up!" But no one came.

So Cheeky Chick carried on looking.
He searched carefully all through the
farmyard, through the vegetable patch and
along the hedgerow at the edge of the field.
He even looked in the haystack, which
took a very long time, but there was no sign
of his brothers and sisters to be found
amongst the hay.

By now it was getting dark, and Cheeky

Chick was feeling scared and lonely.

"It's no use," he said to himself. "I'll have

to go home." He hurried to the henhouse

and opened the door. "Surprise!" came

a loud chorus. His brothers and sisters

had been hiding there all along! It was

a long time before Cheeky Chick played

tricks on them again.

BUNNIES

Baby bunnies are called kittens, and live
with their mothers in a deep burrow, which
she digs underground. As soon as they are

old enough, the little bunnies come out to play in the sunshine, chasing each other through the fields and meadows, their fluffy white tails bouncing as they hop happily along.

EASTER BUNNIES

It was Easter and the naughty bunnies
had hidden eggs for the animals to find.
How they chuckled when they saw the
farm cat shaking the water from her fur.
She had been searching by the pond
and had fallen in!

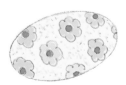

The bunnies giggled as they watched the hens
shooing the pig away from the henhouse.
"They're not in here!" the hens clucked.

Next the little bunnies hurried to the
meadow, where all the sheep were
making a great fuss.

"We've found the Easter eggs!" cried
the sheep, pointing behind a tree.
"Those are toadstools!" laughed the
bunnies. "Keep looking!" By now, the
animals had searched high and low.
"We give up!" said Daisy, the cow.

"Here's a clue," said the bunnies.
"Where do you find eggs?"
"In a nest," answered Mrs Goose.
"And what do you make a nest with?"
asked the bunnies.

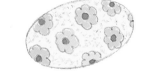

"Straw!" said the horse.
"They must be in the haystack!"
The animals rushed to the field and
there, hidden in the haystack, was a
pile of lovely Easter eggs.
What a feast they had!

BUNNY TAILS

Bunnies come in all different colours and sizes. Some have long ears and some have floppy ears. But all bunnies have fluffy tails. All except Alfie, that is. He had no tail at all and his friends teased him badly. "Never mind, dear," said his mummy. "I love you, tail or no tail."

But Alfie did mind and at night he cried himself to sleep. Then one night he dreamt he met a fairy and told her all about his problem. "A little fairy magic will soon

fix that!" said the fairy. She took some dandelion clocks and sewed them together to make a lovely fluffy tail. "Turn around!" she said and fixed it in place in a flash.

Alfie woke with a start. "If only my dream could come true," he thought sadly and looked down at his back. And there, to his astonishment, was a fine fluffy white tail!

"I'm a real bunny at last!" he said proudly, running off to show his new tail to his friends.

HOME SWEET HOME

Bella Bunny looked at the sweet green grass growing in the meadow on the far side of the stream. She was tired of eating the rough grass that grew near her burrow. "I'm going to cross the stream!" she said to her brothers and sisters, pointing to a fallen branch that lay across it.

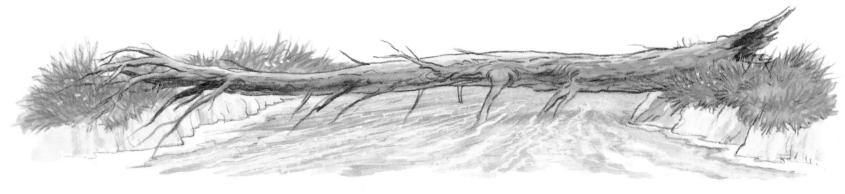

Bella bounced safely across the branch
and was soon eating the sweet, juicy grass
on the other side of the stream.
Her brothers and sisters thought she was

very brave and wondered if they should follow. But just then, they saw a sly fox creeping up behind Bella through the grass! "Look out!" they called.

Bella turned to see the fox just in time!
She leapt back onto the branch, but she
was in such a hurry that she slipped and
fell into the stream. Luckily Becky Beaver
had been watching and she pulled
Bella safely to the other side.
"Home sweet home!" gasped Bella.
And she ran off to join her brothers and
sisters, vowing never to leave home again.

ONE BAD BUNNY

Barney was a very bad bunny. He liked
playing tricks on his friends. Barney hid
Squirrel's nut store and it took him all day to
find it. He put sticky honey on Badger's
walking stick and Badger was chased by bees.
And he put black paint on Mole's glasses, so
poor Mole got even more lost than usual!

"It's time we taught that bad bunny a lesson!" said Badger crossly. So that night, while Barney was sleeping, Mole and Badger dug a big hole. Squirrel climbed up to the treetops and fetched some branches to put

over the hole and they covered it with grass.
They set a big juicy carrot on top, then hid
behind the trees to wait.

The next morning, Barney came bouncing out of his burrow, spotted the juicy carrot and jumped straight into the trap! "Help!" he cried, from the bottom of the hole. The others appeared. "We tricked you!" they laughed. They only let Barney out when he promised to stop playing tricks. And from then on he was a very good bunny indeed.

KITTENS

A mother cat usually gives birth to a litter of
4-6 kittens. When they are born they are
blind and helpless, but very soon they are up

and about, investigating their new home.
Kittens are full of curiosity, and full of mischief,
so Mummy keeps a close eye on them in case
their adventures lead them into trouble!

KATY AND THE BUTTERFLY

As Katy Kitten lay dozing happily in the sun, something tickled her nose. She opened an eye and saw a butterfly hovering above her whiskers. She tapped at it with her soft paw, but it fluttered away. Katy sprang after it and landed with a howl in a bed of thistles, but the butterfly had gone.

"I'll catch that butterfly!" she said, crossly.

Katy chased the butterfly down the garden towards the stream, where it settled on the branch of a tree. She climbed up into the tree after it, higher and higher, but every time she

came near, the butterfly simply flew away.
By now, Katy had climbed so high that she
realised she was quite stuck! Nervously,
she looked down at the stream swirling below her.

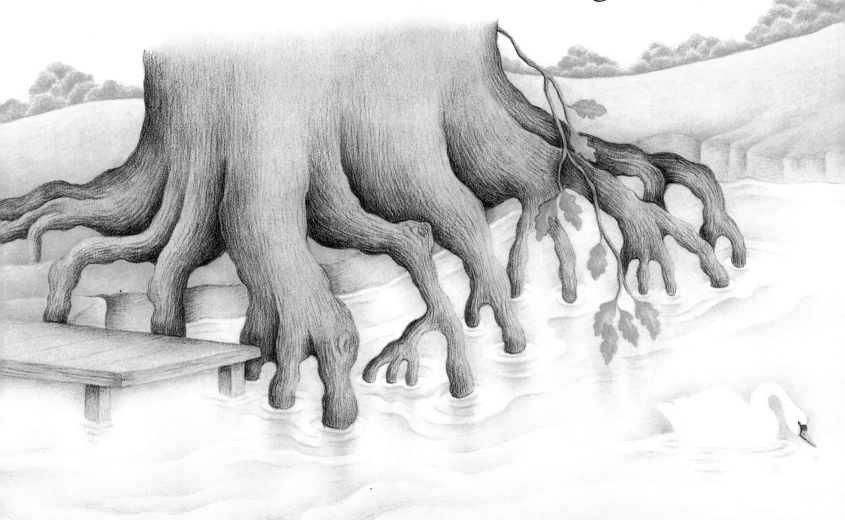

Just then, the butterfly fluttered past her nose.

Without thinking, Katy swiped at it with her paw.

But as she did so, she lost her balance and

went tumbling down through the tree, landing

with a great SPLASH! in the water below.

"Help!" cried Katy, waving her paws wildly.

Luckily she caught hold of a branch hanging

over the stream and clambered onto the bank.

Katy arrived home, cold, wet and limping.
Her fur was tangled and she was scratched all
over. She curled up in front of the fire, feeling
exhausted and started to doze. Just then, she
felt something tugging at her whiskers.

She opened one eye and saw a little mouse. "Oh, no, I've done enough chasing for one day, thank you," said Katy. And with that, she simply closed her eyes, fell fast asleep, and dreamt about chasing butterflies!

ONE DARK NIGHT

Paws tiptoed out into the dark farmyard.
Mummy had told him to stay in the barn until
he was old enough to go out at night. But he
was impatient. He had not gone far when
something brushed past his ears. He froze,
as the fur on his neck began to rise. To his relief
it was only a bat — plenty of those in the barn.

A loud hoot echoed through the trees —
"Tu-whit, tu-whoo," and a great dark shape
swooped down and snatched something up.
"Just an owl," Paws told himself. "Some of
those in the barn too. Nothing to be afraid of!"

Creeping nervously on into the darkness, he wondered if this was such a good idea after all. Strange rustlings came from every corner and he jumped as the old pig gave a loud grunt close by.

Then, all of a sudden Paws froze in his tracks.
Beneath the henhouse two eyes glinted in the
darkness, as they came creeping towards him.
This must be the fox Mummy had warned him of!
But to his amazement he saw it was Mummy!
"Back to the barn!" she said sternly and Paws
happily did as he was told. Maybe he would wait
until he was older to go out at night, after all!

SNOWBALL'S SURPRISE

Snowball was a pretty little kitten, with long white fur, just like a fluffy ball of snow! She loved the snow, because it made her almost invisible, and then she could play all kinds of naughty tricks. She would hide in a snowdrift, and jump out on Mrs Badger as she hurried home, or creep up on the little bunnies and pull their powderpuff tails.

But the other animals were fed up with Snowball's tricks. It was time someone played a trick on her...
Early one day, Snowball crept into the garden and hid in the snowy pine tree.

She started to miaow loudly, keeping her eyes fixed on Percy Pup's kennel. Soon he would come out to chase her, and then she would shake the snowy branch all over him! But someone else was also hiding in the tree...

It was Snowy Owl! He guessed what
Snowball was planning, and waited until
Percy pup appeared. Then, with a great flap
of his wings, and a loud "Tu-whit-tu-whoo!",
he sprang out on Snowball, who tumbled out
of the tree in surprise! She landed right in
front of Percy, who chased her all around the
garden. It was a long time before Snowball
tried playing tricks again!

CHALK AND CHEESE

Chalk and Cheese were as different as two kittens can be. Chalk was a fluffy white kitten, who liked dishes of cream and lazing in the sun. Cheese was a rough, tough black kitten, who liked chewing on fish tails and climbing trees. Their mother puzzled over her odd little pair of kittens, but she loved them both the same.

One day, Cheese climbed high up on the barn and got stuck. "Help!" he cried to his sister. "I don't like climbing!" she said, opening one eye. "If only you were more like me!" said Cheese. "You'd be able to help!"

"If only you were more like me," said Chalk, "you wouldn't have got stuck in the first place!" And with that she went back to sleep. Just then, the farm dog came by. Chalk sprang up as he gave a loud bark and began to chase her.

"Help!" she cried to Cheese, up on the barn. "I'm stuck, remember?" he cried. "You shouldn't lie where dogs can chase you." Then Mummy appeared. She swiped the dog away with her claws, then climbed up and rescued Cheese.

"If only you were more like me," she said, "you'd keep out of danger and look after each other."

And from then on, that's just what they did.

THE DISAPPEARING TRICK

Like all little kittens, Smoky was very playful.
One day, she was chasing her ball, when it
rolled under the fence and into the garden on the
other side. Forgetting Mummy's warnings about
the mean dog who lived there, Smoky
squeezed through the fence, just in time to see
her ball disappear into a hole in the grass...

Smoky looked down into the hole, but it was
very deep and there was no sign of the ball.
Just then, she heard a low growl, and turned
to see an angry dog snarling at her.
In a flash, she scrambled into the hole,

with the dog's sharp teeth snapping at her heels. She squeezed down a long tunnel and into a little room at the bottom. "Hello!" said Rabbit, handing Smoky the ball. "You must be looking for this!"

Smoky was amazed to find she was in Rabbit's burrow. She told him about the angry dog. "Don't worry," said Rabbit, "we'll trick him!" He dug a new tunnel and in no time they were back in Smoky's garden. "Over here!" Rabbit called through the fence to the poor dog still guarding the hole! How the two friends laughed to see the puzzled look on his face.

DUCKLINGS

All along rivers and around ponds, fluffy little ducklings appear in nests at the start of spring. They hatch out from their eggs, and

are soon swimming along behind their mother
in a long line, eager to meet all the other
riverside folk, and explore the exciting sights
and sounds of their watery world.

DANNY DUCKLING IN TROUBLE

"Stay still so I can count!" quacked Mummy Duck crossly, as the little ducklings splashed about. "Just as I thought, Danny's missing again. We'd better go and look for him!" It was the third time that week Danny Duckling had got lost. He liked to swim at the end of the line and often got left behind. But this time he was in trouble…

Earlier that day, Danny had been following
along through the reeds when his foot caught in
something beneath the water.
"Bother!" he quacked as he tried to pull it free.

He ducked into the water and saw that his foot was tangled in an old fishing net held fast in the mud. "Help!" he cried to the others, but they were already too far away to hear.

The more Danny struggled, the tighter the net gripped his foot. "Help!" he quacked, flapping his fluffy little wings. Luckily, Freya Frog heard his cries and dived under the water to try and free him, but it was no use. "I'll go and get help," she said, swimming off. "Hurry!" Danny called after her. The tide was coming in and the river was rising fast!

By the time Freya returned with Wally Water
Rat, the water was covering Danny's back.
"I'm going to be pulled under!" cried Danny.
"Don't worry," said Wally. "We'll save you!"
In no time at all, Wally's sharp teeth nibbled

through the net, and Danny bobbed back to
the surface just as his Mummy appeared.
"Thank goodness you're safe," said Mummy.
"But from now on swim at the front of the line."
And that is just what Danny did.

ALL AT SEA!

It was a lovely spring day when Dippy Duckling peeked out of her warm nest at the shimmering river. How cool and inviting the water looked. Soon she was swimming along happily, calling out to all the animals that lived on the riverbank as she went by. She didn't realise how fast or how far the current was carrying her as she swept along past forests and fields.

As Dippy floated on enjoying the warm sun on her back Sally Seagull flew by squawking loudly. "I've never seen a bird like that on the river before," thought Dippy, in surprise.

Then just as she came round a great bend in the river she saw the wide shining ocean spread out in front of her! Dippy began to shake with terror — she was going to be swept out to sea!

She started to paddle furiously against the tide,

but it was no use. The current was too strong.

Just then, a friendly face popped up nearby.

It was Ollie Otter. He was very surprised to find

Dippy so far from home. "Climb on my back,"

he said. Soon his strong legs were pulling them

back up the river and safely home.

"Thank you, Ollie," said Dippy. "Without you,

I'd be all at sea!"

FOREVER FRIENDS

Daisy Duckling had lots of friends but her best friend of all was Glenda Gosling. Every day they played together, chasing each other through the reeds. "When I grow up, I'll be a beautiful swan like my mummy!" said Glenda. "And I'll be a dull little brown duck," said Daisy. She worried that Glenda would only want to play with her pretty swan friends when she grew up.

Then one day, they were playing hide and seek
when something dreadful happened.
While Daisy hid amongst some large dock leaves,
a sly fox crept up and snatched her in his mouth!

Before she had time to quack he was heading for his lair. But Glenda been watching. Without hesitating she rushed after the fox and caught the tip of his long tail in her sharp beak.

As the fox spun round, she pecked him hard on the nose. His mouth dropped open and Daisy fell out. Now he was really mad and rushed at them. But Mrs Duck and Mrs Swan flew at him hissing furiously and off he ran. Daisy couldn't thank them enough. "That's what friends are for!" said Glenda. And Mrs Swan and Mrs Duck, who were the best of friends, could not agree more.

LIKE A DUCK TO WATER

Mrs Duck swam proudly across the farm pond followed by a line of fluffy ducklings. Hidden in the safety of the nest Dozy Duckling peeked out and watched them go. He wished he was brave enough to go with them but he was afraid of the water! Instead, he pretended to be asleep, and Mrs Duck told the others to leave him alone.

When they returned that night they told him tales of all the scary animals they had met by the pond. "There's a big thing with hot breath called Horse," said Dotty. "There's a huge smelly pink thing called Pig," said Dickie.

"But worst of all," said Doris, "there's a great grey bird, called Heron. Pig says he gobbles up little ducklings for breakfast!" At that all the little ducklings squawked with fear and excitement.

Next morning, Mrs Duck hurried the ducklings out for their morning parade.

Dozy kept his eyes shut until they had gone then looked up to see a great grey bird towering over him! He leapt into the water crying, "Help, wait for me!" But the others started laughing! "It's a trick! Heron won't eat you. We just wanted you to come swimming. And you've taken to it like a duck to water!"

PUPPIES

A mother dog usually gives birth to 6~7
puppies at a time, and they are called a litter.
Puppies are very playful, and love chasing

each other as they rough and tumble, nipping each other with their sharp little puppy teeth. They have heaps of energy, which they use to bound about, exploring the world around them.

SMELLY PUP

All the animals were gathered in the barn.
"It has come to our attention," said Mrs
Hen to Smelly Pup, "that you are in need
of a bath. You haven't had one all summer.
Even the pigs are complaining!"
Smelly Pup just laughed. "Me? Take a bath?
That'll be the day!" he said, and off he went.

Outside Smelly Pup strolled through the
farmyard, muttering, "What a crazy idea.
I'm a dog. I do dog things... like chasing cats!"
The farm cat leapt up hissing as Smelly Pup

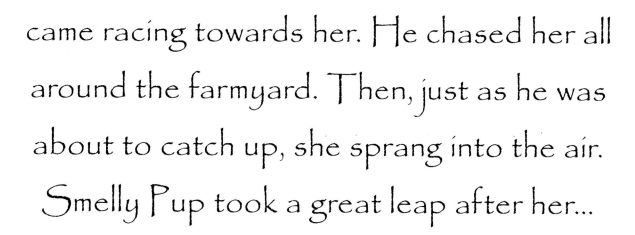

came racing towards her. He chased her all around the farmyard. Then, just as he was about to catch up, she sprang into the air. Smelly Pup took a great leap after her...

... and landed in the pond with a SPLASH!
"Silly Pup!" smirked the cat from a nearby tree.
The ducks quacked as he spluttered and
splashed, chasing them through the shallows!
The water felt cool and refreshing on his fur.
After a while, he came out and rolled on the
nice muddy bank. "That was fun," he said.
"Maybe I could get used to baths after all!"

CHASING TAILS

Barney had been chasing his tail all
morning. Round and round he went, until he
made himself feel quite dizzy.
"Can't you find something useful to do?"
asked the cat, from where she sat watching
him on the fence.
"What? Like chasing lazy cats?" said Barney,
as he leapt towards her, barking fiercely.

Later, as he trotted around the farmyard,
Barney thought about what the cat had said.
He wished he could be more useful, but he
was only a little pup. When he grew up,
he would be a fine, useful farm dog, like his mum.

Just then, he rounded the barn, and there
in front of him waved a big bushy tail...
"Here's a tail I can catch!" thought Barney
playfully, and he sprang forward and sank
his sharp little puppy teeth into it!

Now, the tail belonged to a sly fox, who was
about to pounce on Mrs Hen and her
chicks! The fox yelped in surprise, and ran
away across the fields.

"Ooh, Barney, you saved us!" cried Mrs Hen.
The cat was watching from the fence.
"Maybe all that practice chasing tails has
come in useful after all!" she said.

PUPPY PLAYTIME

Nipper and Scratch rolled over and over
on the ground, yelping as they nipped each
other with their sharp little puppy teeth.
"That's enough now boys," said Mummy.
"We're only playing!" protested Scratch.
"Well, don't play so roughly,' said Mummy.
"One of you might get hurt!"
"We'll be careful," promised Nipper.

Later that day, Scratch was sniffing at some long grass, when Nipper jumped out on him from behind the old elm tree. "Got you!" he yapped, snapping at Scratch's tail! The two little pups

went tumbling through the grass, growling and fighting, before falling head over heels down the steep bank that led to the stream, and landing in a crumpled heap at the water's edge.

Nipper jumped up, puffing and panting,

ready to carry on playing. But Scratch

lay quite still, his eyes shut tight.

"Are you alright, Scratch?" asked Nipper,

feeling worried. "Say something!"

"I think mummy was right!" groaned Scratch,

rolling over and opening one eye. "This fighting

game hurts. From now on, let's stick to chase!"

And with that, the two little pups chased

each other all down the stream.

BONE CRAZY!

Alfie sat in his basket chewing on a large
bone. Mmm! It tasted good. When he had
chewed it for long enough, he took it down to
the bottom of the garden, to bury it in his
favourite spot, beneath the old oak tree.
He didn't see next door's dog, Ferdy,
watching him through a hole in the fence.

The next day, when Alfie went to dig up his bone, it was gone! He dug all around, but it was nowhere to be found. Just then, he spied a trail of muddy paw prints leading to the fence, and he realised what had happened.

Alfie was too big to fit through the fence and get his bone back, so he thought of a plan, instead! Next day he buried another bone. This time, he knew Ferdy was watching him.

Later he hid and watched as Ferdy crept into the garden and started to dig up the bone. Just then, Ferdy yelped in pain. The bone had bitten his nose! He flew across the garden and through the fence leaving the bone behind. Alfie's friend Mole crept out from where the bone was buried. How the two friends laughed at their trick! And from then, Ferdy always kept safely to his side of the fence!

ONE STORMY NIGHT

It was Patch's first night outside in his smart new kennel. He snuggled down on his warm blanket and watched as the skies grew dark.

Before long he fell fast asleep.

As he slept, big spots of rain began to fall.

A splash of water dripped from the kennel roof on to his nose, which started to twitch.

Just then, there was a great crash and a bright flash of light lit up the sky. Patch woke with a start and was on his feet at once, growling and snarling. "It's just a silly old storm," he told himself.

"Nothing to scare a fearless farm dog like me!"
But as the lightning flashed again, he saw a
great shadow looming against the barn.
Patch gulped. Whatever could it be?

Patch peered into the darkness, but could see nothing through the rain. Just then, the sky lit up once more, and sure enough, there was the shadow, but larger and closer than before! Patch began to bark furiously, trying to act braver than he felt. Next time the lightning flashed, there was no sign of the shadow.

"I soon scared that monster away!" he thought.

But as Patch settled back down in his cosy kennel, the sky outside lit up once more, and there in the doorway towered the monster! "Just checking you're okay in the storm," said

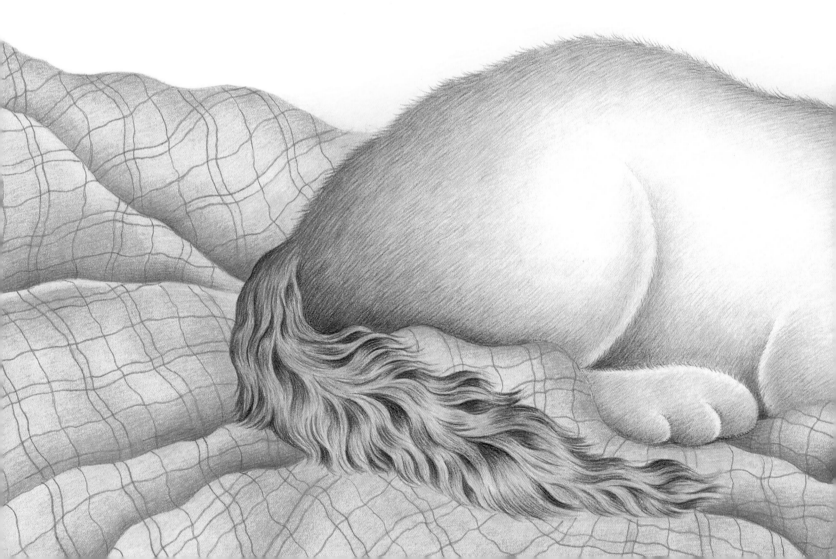

Mummy, giving Patch a gentle lick on the ear.
"A fearless farm dog like me?" said Patch.
"Of course I am!" But as the storm raged
on, he snuggled up close to her all the same!

BEARS

Bears live in deep caves in the hills and
mountains, called dens. In the spring, the
baby bear cubs venture out to discover

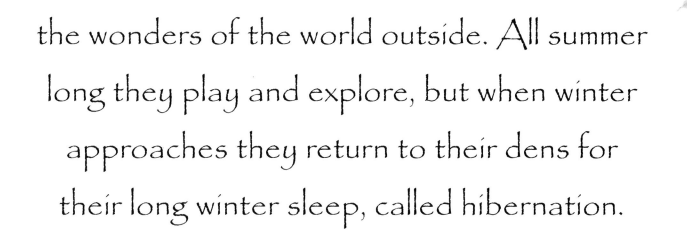

the wonders of the world outside. All summer long they play and explore, but when winter approaches they return to their dens for their long winter sleep, called hibernation.

HONEY BEAR AND THE BEES

One day, as Honey Bear woke from her dreams, her furry little nose started to twitch with excitement. She could smell her favourite thing in the world — sweet, yummy honey! The smell was coming from a hollow tree stump nearby. She padded over and dipped in a large paw. How delicious the sweet, sticky honey tasted!

Honey Bear dipped her paw in again and
again, digging deep into the tree stump to
reach more of the lovely sticky honey.
This was the life! In fact, she dug so deep

that when she tried to take her great paw out,
she found it was stuck fast! Just then, she heard
a loud buzzing noise and looked up to see a huge
swarm of angry bees returning to their hive!

Poor Honey Bear hollered as the bees
flew around, stinging her all over! She tugged
and tugged and at last she pulled her paw free.
The angry bees chased her all the way to the
river where she sat cooling her burning skin.
Just then an irresistible smell reached her furry
nose. It was coming from a hollow tree nearby.
"Mmm, honey!" said Honey Bear. "I'll just go
and take a look!"

Baby Bear Finds a Friend

Baby Bear stretched as he woke from his long winter sleep. He took a deep breath of fresh spring air and smiled at the warm sun on his back. He was bursting with energy. Now all he needed was someone to play with.

"Come and play with me," he called to Owl.

"I only play at night!" said Owl, sleepily.

Nearby some little bunnies were playing. Baby Bear bounded over to join the fun, but Mrs Rabbit shooed him away. "Your paws will hurt my babies," she said. "You can't play with them."

Next he climbed up to see if Squirrel would play with him, but Squirrel told him to go away. "I'm trying to make a nest," said Squirrel, crossly, "and you are shaking the tree!"

Baby Bear wandered down to the river, where
some beavers were hard at work building a dam.
"Come and play with me," called Baby Bear.
But the beavers were too busy. So he sat
watching Kingfisher diving into the water.
"That looks like fun!" he said, jumping in
with a splash! "Go away!" said Kingfisher.
"You're disturbing the fish!"

By now Baby Bear was feeling fed up and tired. He lay down in a hollow and closed his eyes. Then, just as he was drifting to sleep, a voice said, "Will you come and play with me?"

He opened his eyes to see another bear cub.
Baby Bear smiled. "I'm too tired to play now,"
he said. "But I'll play with you tomorrow!"
And from then on, he was never lonely again.

One Snowy Day

One snowy day, Old Bear poked his nose out of his den, and looked at the deep snow that had fallen while he slept. "I'll take a stroll in the woods," he said. Off he went, his great paws padding along, as big white snowflakes tickled his nose. How he loved the snow! He walked far into the woods, deep in thought, and quite forgot to look where he was going.

After a while, Old Bear stopped and looked around. To his dismay, he realised he was quite lost. Then he spied the trail of pawprints behind him. "Ho, ho!" he chuckled. "I'm not lost at all! I can follow my pawprints home!"

And thinking what a clever old bear he was, he carried on walking, until at last he began to feel tired. "I'll just take a rest," he said to himself. He closed his eyes, and soon fell fast asleep. Meanwhile, the snow kept on falling...

By the time Old Bear woke up his trail of pawprints had disappeared! "Now I'll never find my way home!" he groaned. Then, he noticed an old tree stump nearby. "That looks familiar. And so does that fallen log over there. If I'm not mistaken, I've walked in a big circle, and ended up at home!" he chuckled, turning towards his den. "What a clever old bear I am, after all!"

THE SMART BEAR AND THE FOOLISH BEAR

It was the start of winter. The first snow had fallen, and the lake had begun to freeze. It was nearly time for all the bears to start their winter sleep. But there was one foolish bear who wasn't ready to sleep yet. "I'll just catch one more fish," he told himself, "to keep me going through winter." And although he knew it was dangerous, he crept out onto the icy lake.

He lay down on his tummy, and broke a hole
in the ice. He could see lots of fish swimming
in the water below. He dipped his paw into
the hole, and scooped out a fish in a flash!

But the foolish little bear was so excited he
leapt up, shouting, "I caught one!" With a
great crack, the ice gave way beneath him,
and he fell into the freezing water!

Luckily a smart little bear cub heard his cries, and rushed to help. He found a fallen log and pushed it over the ice. The foolish bear grabbed it, and pulled himself to safety, still holding the fish. "How can I thank you?" he asked. "That fish would do nicely," said the smart little bear, and he strolled away to start his winter's sleep.

The End